ALSO AVAILABLE

Book 2: *Amina Banana and the Formula for Winning*

Amina Banana

AND THE FORMULA FOR FRIENDSHIP

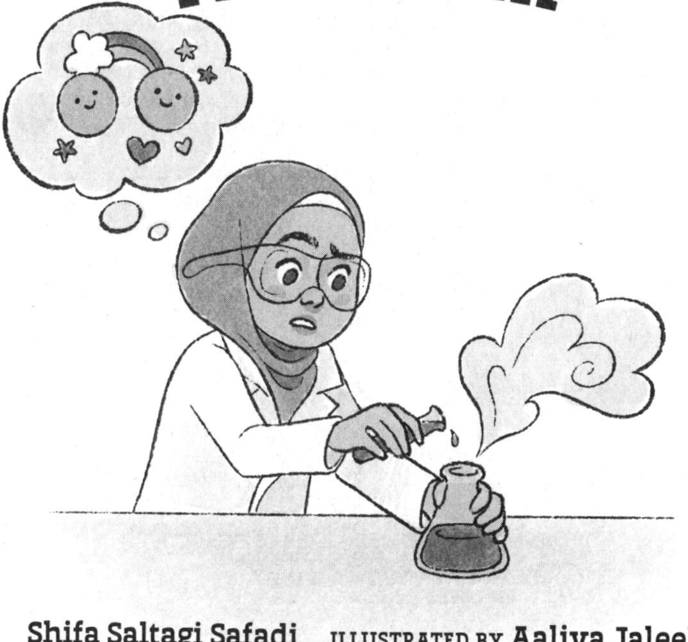

Shifa Saltagi Safadi ILLUSTRATED BY Aaliya Jaleel

putnam

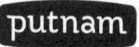

G. P. PUTNAM'S SONS

G. P. PUTNAM'S SONS
An imprint of Penguin Random House LLC
1745 Broadway, New York, New York 10019

First published in the United States of America by G. P. Putnam's Sons,
an imprint of Penguin Random House LLC, 2025

Text copyright © 2025 by Shifa Saltagi Safadi
Illustrations copyright © 2025 by Aaliya Jaleel
Amina Banana and the Formula for Winning excerpt text copyright © 2025 by
Shifa Saltagi Safadi
Amina Banana and the Formula for Winning excerpt illustrations copyright © 2025
by Aaliya Jaleel

Penguin Random House values and supports copyright. Copyright fuels
creativity, encourages diverse voices, promotes free speech, and creates a
vibrant culture. Thank you for buying an authorized edition of this book and for
complying with copyright laws by not reproducing, scanning, or distributing
any part of it in any form without permission. You are supporting writers and
allowing Penguin Random House to continue to publish books for every reader.
Please note that no part of this book may be used or reproduced in any manner
for the purpose of training artificial intelligence technologies or systems.

G. P. Putnam's Sons is a registered trademark of Penguin Random House LLC.
The Penguin colophon is a registered trademark of Penguin Books Limited.

Visit us online at PenguinRandomHouse.com.

Library of Congress Cataloging-in-Publication Data is available.

ISBN 9780593699225 (hardcover)

ISBN 9780593699140 (paperback)

1st Printing

Printed in the United States of America

LSCC

Design by Kristie Radwilowicz
Text set in Franziska Pro

This book is a work of fiction. Any references to historical events, real people,
or real places are used fictitiously. Other names, characters, places, and events
are products of the author's imagination, and any resemblance to actual events
or places or persons, living or dead, is entirely coincidental.

The authorized representative in the EU for product safety and compliance is
Penguin Random House Ireland, Morrison Chambers, 32 Nassau Street, Dublin
D02 YH68, Ireland, https://eu-contact.penguin.ie.

To my parents, who uprooted their lives
from Syria in search for a better future.
You always grounded us in love and faith
and helped us flower in new soil.
May Allah reward you!

—Shifa

For Hayaa

—**Aaliya Jaleel**

CONTENTS

Chapter 1: **GETTING READY** 1

Chapter 2: **FUL BEFORE SCHOOL** 7

Chapter 3: **MIX-UP IN THE HALL** 15

Chapter 4: **TORNADO BRAIN** 24

Chapter 5: **LUNCHTIME** 30

Chapter 6: **SCIENCE, FINALLY!** 38

Chapter 7: **AMERICAN APPLE PIE** 47

Chapter 8: **A FUL FOOL** 58

Chapter 9: **A MASJID REVELATION** 68

Chapter 10: **AMINA BANANA** 76

Chapter 11: **THE FINAL INGREDIENT** ... 85

EXTRAS!

THE STEPS OF MRS. JAMES'S SCIENTIFIC METHOD 95

AN EXPERIMENT ON SMELL AND TASTE 97

AMINA'S FUL MDAMAS RECIPE 100

A NOTE FROM THE AUTHOR 103

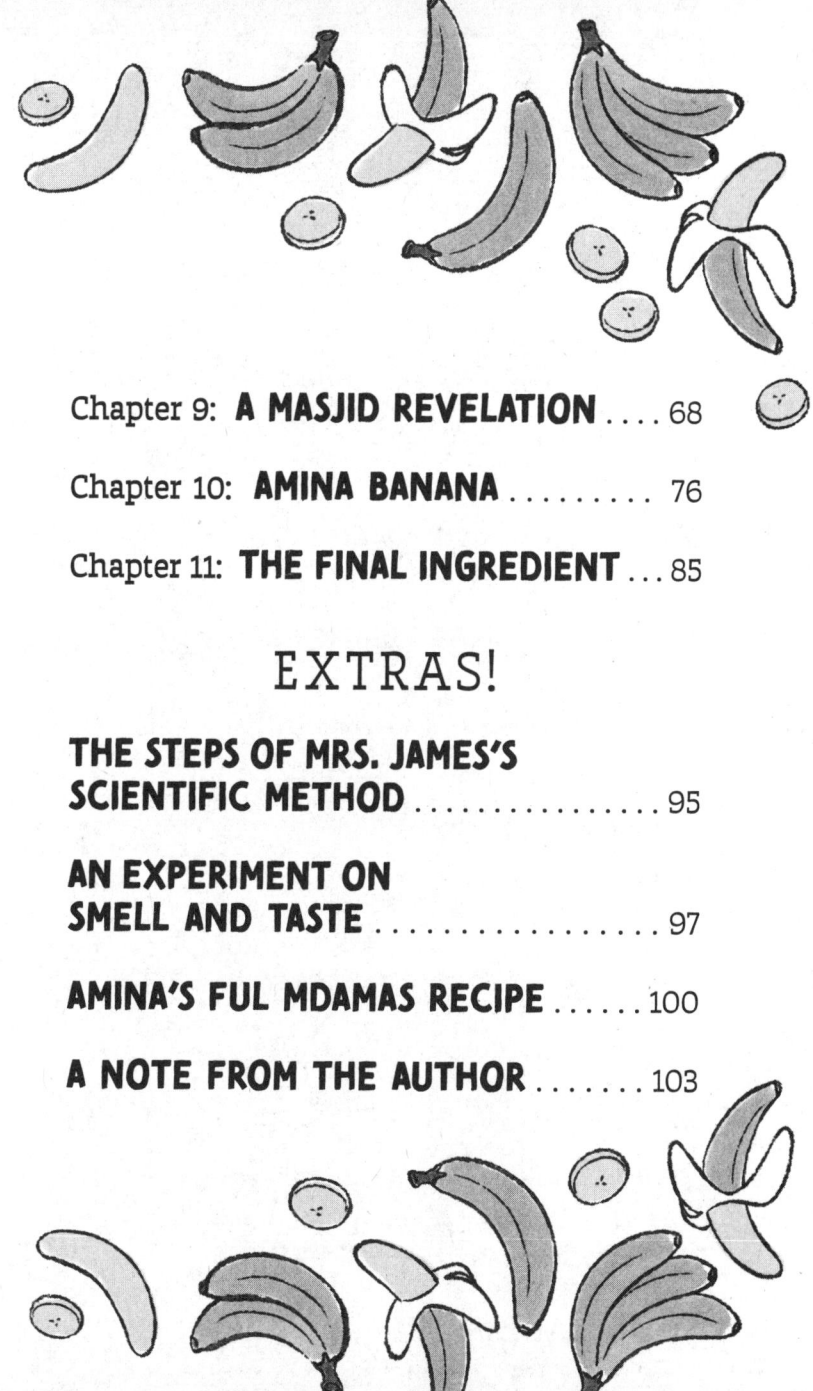

★ 1 ★

GETTING READY

First day of American school!

My stomach tickles me as I brush my teeth with the sparkly blue toothpaste that tastes like candy. Mama said I shouldn't swallow it, so I try not to.

But a toothpaste grin fills my face as I think of my best friend. Judy would have licked the toothpaste tube, no matter what the rules say.

My smile fades when I remember Judy's still in Syria. This is the first school year since preschool I start without her.

I wonder if she is getting ready for school today too.

I miss walking with her, singing Arabic rhymes in tune to our steps, even if we had to sometimes dodge crumbling rubble from buildings destroyed by the war.

We always made it to school hand in hand.

I spit out the paste, rinse my mouth, and

splash water on my face. I hope third grade won't be hard, especially since I'm starting two weeks late. But I hadn't even been in America when school began.

Sometimes, when I close my eyes, it feels like I'm back on a rocky, flimsy boat, floating over dark waters, my stomach bobbing up and down. Or standing in long lines under the glaring sun, my spirit melting as I watch Baba fill out the same papers over and over.

He had called it traveling, but leaving Syria wasn't a fun vacation, no matter how much I tried to pretend otherwise.

And I couldn't make friends when we kept moving from country to country.

I hop over the creaking floorboards on the way back to my bedroom. I pick up my new bookbag and start filling it carefully. Our refugee caseworker, Ms. Lee, had helped me check off all the items on my supplies list, one by one.

Markers, pencils, pink erasers, notebooks, folders, and glittery purple glue sticks. My favorite purchase, though, is the bright yellow bookbag.

The color of bananas is the color of pure happiness.

"Now you're all ready to be an American student," Ms. Lee had told me. Ms. Lee was almost right. The supplies list helped me prepare what I needed for my first day. But I wish there was a list on how to make American friends too.

Mama had clasped Ms. Lee's hands to thank her over and over for helping us, but she kept repeating, "It's the least I can do."

She found us a house to live in, took us to get clothes, signed me and my brother up for school, and helped Baba get a used car so he can go to work, so I'm not sure why she said it was only a little help!

I open my rickety dresser drawer, careful not to pull too fast (or else it will fall on my feet!), and pick the brightest, frilliest, yellowiest dress I own. When I told Ms. Lee yellow was my favorite color, she made sure to search through all the aisles at Goodwill with me until I had a full yellow wardrobe.

I twirl and look at my reflection in the dresser mirror. And although my nerves are still popping like little bubbles, I smile.

I'm ready!

2

FUL BEFORE SCHOOL

I pass Sami's room, but his bed's already empty. I see clothes strewn all over the carpet and I know he must have been worried about what to wear to school.

Mama said high school is a high amount of school work, but Baba said it's called that because of how high Sami styles his hair. I hide a smile when I remember how much we giggled at the silly joke.

I skip down the stairs, my yellow bookbag bouncing on my back.

"Jahze?" Baba smiles at me from the bench where he's putting on his shoes.

"I think so," I tell him in Arabic. I remember my school in Syria. I miss my books, my teacher's warm smile, and the smell of the yellow flowers outside the school building.

But mostly, I miss science class. "Do you think they do science experiments here?"

Baba laughs. "I'm sure they do!"

My stomach tickles me again. "I hope I make friends."

"It'll be easy for you," Baba says, kissing my

forehead before he leaves for work. "Just like science."

His words give me an idea. Science is made up of formulas, and formulas make solutions, so what I really need is a special formula. Something that will help me fit in.

I zip open my bookbag, pull out a notebook, and write FORMULA FOR MAKING AMERICAN FRIENDS right at the top.

After a few minutes of writing, I stop and smile.

Speak English perfectly + Wear a perfect outfit + Be a good student + Eat American food = American Friends!

Perfect.

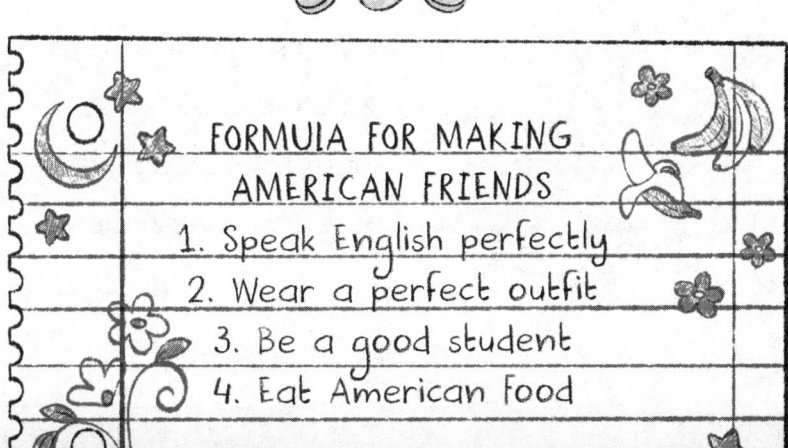

I walk into the kitchen and inhale the familiar garlicky-lemon smell of ful. Baba must have woken up really early to cook breakfast.

"Do American beans taste like Syrian ones?" I ask Mama. They sure smell the same.

She looks up from the pile of books on the kitchen table in front of her. "Cooking is the same everywhere, Amina. You just put the ingredients together and add them in a special formula."

I laugh. That's funny, coming from Mama.

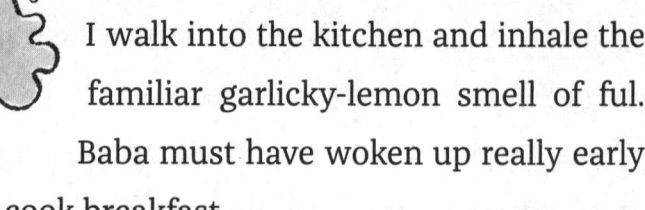

No matter how many formulas she uses, her cooking *always* fails.

Heba squeals from her high chair. She bangs a spoon on her plate, splattering ful everywhere.

She puts a chubby hand in her mouth, takes a taste, and squawks her approval.

It must be yummy if Heba likes it.

But when I say Bismillah and scoop the ful into my mouth with a small piece of pita bread, it tastes different from the breakfast beans I had back home.

I push away my plate.

"Hurry, you don't want to miss the bus," Mama says. I wash my hands and pop a banana in my bag. Bananas were so hard to find in Syria. But here, I could make a pile of them so high at the grocery store, it would be taller than me. I imagine myself falling into a pile of bananas and giggle.

I wrap a yellow hijab around my head and look into the hallway mirror, my grin glowing back at me. The soft cloth feels like a friend, always reminding me that Allah is with me.

"Have a good first day at school, Amina," says Mama in Arabic. "I'll make duaa for you."

I kiss Mama, wave salaam, and walk to the front door, down the rickety wooden steps, and out to the driveway. September leaves crunch underneath my feet, the sound echoing around the cul-de-sac.

Cute little dandelion flowers peek at me through the colorful leaves piled near my bus stop. More yellow.

When I hear the bus approach, I look up. Its

red light blinks at me in hello, and my smile gets wider. Buses here are yellow too!

The shiny sun warms my face and my heart dances. All this yellow must mean today is going to be a great day.

When the bus screeches to a stop and the doors clank open, I climb the black steps and make my way to the back. I sit in an empty spot and put my bookbag next to me. The girl across from me looks up.

"I love your bag," she says, the colorful beads in her hair clinking together. "My name's Crystal. Are you new?"

"Yes. Sank you." I beam at her. Anyone who loves yellow is sure to be nice.

"'Sank'?" A girl sticks her head over from the seat behind me, her perfect brown curls framing the mocking sneer on her face. "Don't you know how to speak English?"

I sink against my seat. I pull out my notebook and cross out number one on my list.

FORMULA FOR MAKING
AMERICAN FRIENDS

1. ~~Speak English perfectly~~

"Cut it out, Tara," I hear Crystal say.

Cut it out? Cutting sounds dangerous. My heart begins to pound, and I slowly put my notebook back into my bookbag and scoot all the way to the window.

✦ 3 ✦

MIX-UP IN THE HALL

When the bus stops at the school entrance, I am stuck to my seat with worry. I already made one mistake. I'm not going to make friends if my formula doesn't work!

I feel a tap on my shoulder. It's Crystal. "Do you know which way to go? What class are you in?"

"Mmmm . . ." I hesitate. Tara's looking at me. I don't want her to make fun of me if I mess up again. What's the best word to ask

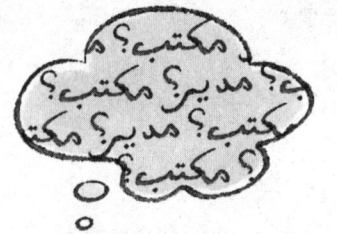

for directions to the maktab? And what's modeer in English?

Crystal laughs. "Don't worry, I don't bite," she says.

Bite? Americans bite each other?

I shake my head quickly. Crystal shrugs. I follow her and Tara off the bus and jump down the steps.

I look up. I still can't believe how huge the building is! So much bigger than my school in Syria, with three levels instead of one, and too many windows to count.

For a moment I wonder:

Can I do this?

I take a deep breath, lift my chin, and walk forward, pushing the doors to the building open.

I step inside the loud halls. Everyone is

shouting, bells are ringing, and students are running. I even see a few paper airplanes being tossed in the air.

And so many doors! In Syria, we had a big courtyard in the middle, and it had a fountain that welcomed us in the morning with a peaceful song of sprinkling water. Everyone filed to class quietly, and dresses and skirts swirled and swayed as everyone in my all-girl school hurried to the classrooms.

But here, I'm the only one wearing a dress. Everyone is wearing . . . jeans? I wonder if that's why the other kids are staring at me. I pull at the yellow fabric and watch it wrinkle, just like my feelings.

I make a mental note to cross out number two on my list.

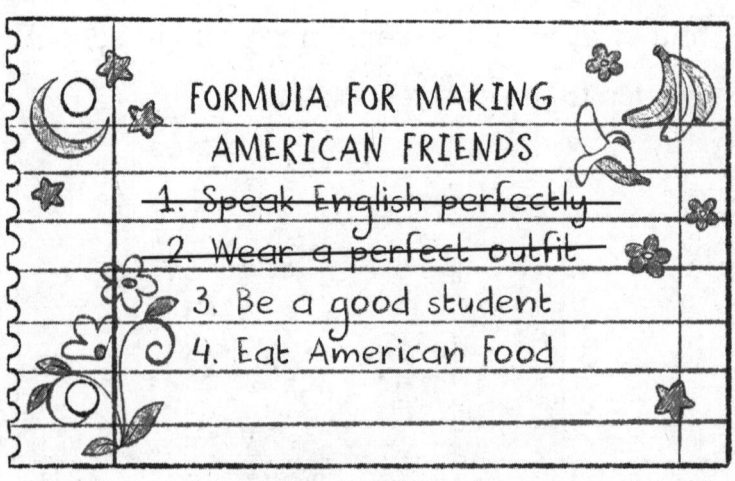

FORMULA FOR MAKING AMERICAN FRIENDS
1. ~~Speak English perfectly~~
2. ~~Wear a perfect outfit~~
3. Be a good student
4. Eat American food

A ringing noise makes me jump. Somehow, students start to move quicker and the noises get louder.

I want to cover my ears, but I press my hands to my side. I can't remember the route Ms. Lee showed me a few days ago.

Within seconds of the loud noise, the hall settles and suddenly it's empty.

I look at the closed doors, wondering which is the principal's office, but they all look the same. Wooden, with a small skinny rectangle right above the door handle. And English words are everywhere, so many that they all just blur together in front of my eyes.

I pick a random door and walk in, but when I step through, a terrible smell hits my nose.

Before I can walk out, a boy sees me. "What are you doing here? This is the boys' restroom!" he shouts. My face burns, and I rush back into the hall. I didn't know! And why would he call the toilets a room for resting, anyways?

I slam straight into someone.

"Am-eena, I've been looking for you. Let's

get you to class," Principal Franklin rattles off. "We've paired you with another student who's Syrian too."

It's AAH-mina, not Am-EEna! Before I can tell him he said my name wrong, he lumbers away, motioning me behind him.

I take a deep breath and hurry behind him to a brightly decorated door. A huge map is taped to it, and I can see names written over different countries. There's one name on top of Syria. *Lana.*

I run a finger over the map and step into my new classroom. Principal Franklin is waiting for me, his foot tapping impatiently.

I look around. The desks all face a whiteboard where a teacher is writing with a black marker. Back home, Judy and I used to share a desk, but here, each student sits at their own, far apart.

It looks kind of lonely.

"This is Mrs. James," Principal Franklin says.

Mrs. James turns from the board. "Welcome to my third-grade class! We're so happy to have you with us." Mrs. James's red curly hair reminds me of Ms. Frizzle of the Magic School Bus series on Spacetoon, the kids' cartoon channel in Syria. The cartoons that only came on when the electricity worked . . . which was very little.

I hope she likes science too.

"Mrs. James will help get you settled." Principal Franklin waves as he leaves the class. I fidget and look at my feet. I'm standing all by myself, right in the middle, and I can feel everyone's eyes on me.

"Would you like to introduce yourself?" Mrs. James asks.

My heart pounds in my ears. I barely manage to mumble my name.

My teacher smiles. "Am-eena is a beautiful name."

Everyone keeps saying my name wrong!

I hear a snicker from the class, but I don't dare turn and see who it is.

Mrs. James straightens. "Listen up, everyone. Please make sure to give a proper welcome to Am-eena. She's new, and it is our responsibility to help make her adjustment easy. I expect you all to be on your best behavior."

I feel my heart settle. American teachers are nice, just like the ones in Syria.

"Take a seat," Mrs. James says. "You're in the empty desk, right next to Lana." I look to where she points. Lana shrinks in her seat, like she wants to disappear, her straight blond hair completely covering her face. On her other side is Crystal, who gives me a huge smile.

I look at the desk in front of my empty one, and gasp. Tara narrows her eyes and scowls at me.

SHE'S in my class too!

⋆ 4 ⋆

Mrs. James starts a lesson in English, and my mind feels like a tornado.

I learned English in Syria, but when my teacher talks superfast about all the rules, I can't follow. What's the difference between *there*, *their*, and *they're*? Why is an *e* silent at times, and why not just take it completely out? Why do some words sound completely the same but their spellings change based on their meanings? Like *fair* and *fare*. Or *sight* and *site*.

I groan in frustration.

Lana isn't any help. When I ask her a question in Arabic, she doesn't answer. When I ask her a question in English, the boy sitting in front of me snorts. "It's not rocket science," he says.

What does science have to do with English? I want to scream.

But I just keep quiet.

And during spelling, I keep writing words and crossing them out until my paper is a huge mess of jumbled letters.

Mrs. James collects our practice tests, but when she takes mine, she looks over it an extra-long second before walking back to her desk.

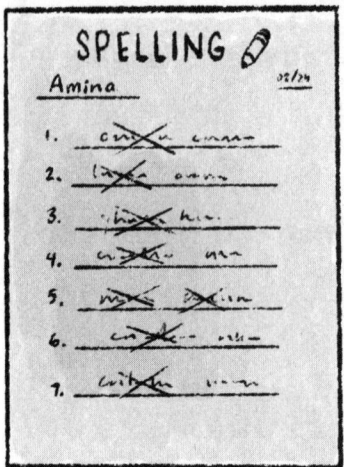

When the rest of the class files out for lunch, she pulls me aside.

"Principal Franklin said we would be giving you a trial period for a month to see how you do," she says, "but I can already tell you're feeling lost."

My shoulders slump and I let out a sigh. I've failed school in America on my first day because I couldn't find my classroom.

I blurt out, "I find class tomorrow. I only lost because the school big."

Mrs. James's eyes crinkle at me. "Not physically lost, dear. I mean that you seemed confused while I was teaching today."

I look at my ungraded spelling test on her desk. I'm pretty sure every single one of my words is spelled wrong.

I should just go back to my desk and pull my notebook out again.

"I believe you would benefit with some extra help," my teacher continues, interrupting

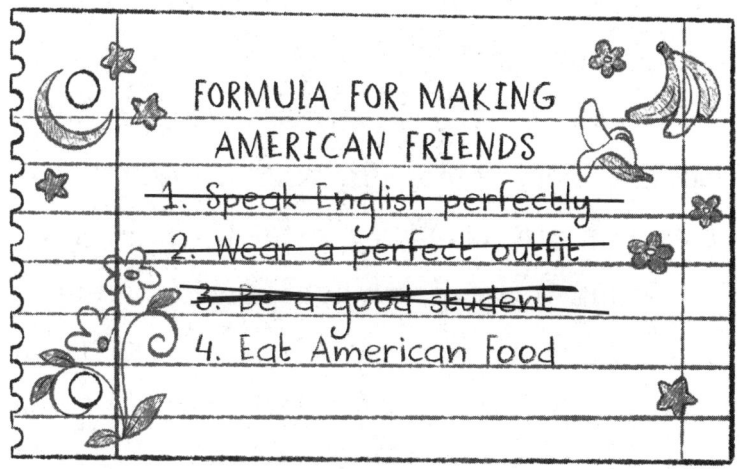

my thoughts. "Just for a little while until you get used to it. I'll go ahead and talk to the librarian about starting your ESL classes."

"What ESL?" I ask.

"English as a Second Language," she says. "Ms. Tanya is great with helping new students get acclimated."

I frown. I don't like the words *second language*. They sound like second place.

"Nothing's wrong with needing extra help," she says. "We all have so much to learn from each other. And only by working together will we taste success."

I touch my tongue with my fingers as I walk out the door. I'm not sure what my American teacher means about the taste of success, but the feeling in my mouth right now is anything but sweet.

★ 5 ★

LUNCHTIME

In the cafeteria, a woman in a white hairnet slaps something smelly on my tray. "No pig?" I whisper to her.

She raises her eyebrows. "You mean pork?" she says loudly. "No, that's pasta salad. Vegetarian." I hear snickers from behind me in the line.

I stare at the rest of the options in silence. Tuna sandwiches that stink, ham and cheese (pig), pizza (with pepperoni, also pig), and Jell-O for dessert (gelatin made of PIG!). I take my

tray to an empty corner table in the cafeteria and slump into a chair.

I poke the mush in front of me. As my fork rises in the air, flecks of beige glop stick to it, and something stringy drops back into my tray. I plop my fork back into the chunky goo and make a face. *This is what Americans eat for lunch?*

I think about the bakery that was next to my school in Syria, where me and Judy would grab fresh zaatar pies. The smell of the dough as it baked in the kiln was like a hug for our noses. And when our hands were filled with the mankushe, we were warmed from head to toe.

Judy and I always shared; she liked the soft center, while I preferred the crisp, tangy edges.

I miss my friend. I tried calling her and sending her emails, but she isn't answering. Baba said it's because the electricity is off most of the day.

I look at my tray and try not to cry.

Tara approaches with a group of other students. I close my eyes, hoping she'll hurry and walk past me.

"You're sitting at our table," she says instead. But there's nowhere for me to go.

"Wanna sit with us?" someone asks.

I whirl around.

It's Lana. My eyes widen—I thought she didn't like me. "Eh taban!" I reply. She doesn't answer, and I follow her to her table.

I sit down, my mouth curving up in response to Crystal's infectious grin. "How do you like our school, Am-eena?" she asks, saying my name wrong again. I look down at my tray of food.

How do you say I-already-failed-my-first-day-of-American-school-and-I-wish-I-were-eating-a-fresh-mankushe-instead-of-gooey-pasta-salad in English?

"Cat got your tongue?" Crystal says. Why would a cat have my tongue? Americans say the strangest things.

A girl with a black bob and twinkling eyes smiles at me. "I'm Su," she says. "I love your scarf." She points to my hijab. "Do you have one in blue? Blue is my favorite color." I run my hands over the soft material of my hijab and beam. My hijabs come in all colors.

I put a spoon of the pasta salad in my mouth and grimace as I swallow. It tastes worse than it looks. If cooking is a science, this experiment is a complete failure. I take out my banana and my stomach settles.

Crystal grins. "I love bananas too, Ameena." I open my mouth to correct the way she

says my name, but then close it. I don't want to offend one of the only girls who's been nice to me.

Lana looks at me. "By the way, I don't understand Arabic," she says. "My grandparents moved here from Syria, but we don't really speak Arabic at home unless Tete and Jido visit. And sometimes at our church."

Oh!

"Ana ismi Fatima." A girl across the table leans over and introduces herself.

A huge smile spreads on my face. "You speak Araby?"

"A little," Fatima says, her brown ringlets a halo around her face. "The imam teaches Arabic at the masjid Sunday school, but sometimes it's hard for me to learn everything."

The girl next to Fatima smirks. "Hebrew's super easy to me."

Lana chuckles. "That's 'cause you're a genius, Hannah." Hannah's ponytail swings back and forth as she laughs. I immediately feel my heart warm toward her. Judy swung her ponytail like that too.

"It's not easy to learn two languages. I still mix up my words, and my parents have been speaking Korean to me my whole life," Su says.

"You guys are awesome for learning two

languages," a girl with red hair and freckles jokes. "I can barely keep track of one!"

I chuckle. The girl winks at me. "I'm Bella."

I look around the table. I guess I'm not the only one struggling.

And somehow, that makes me feel a little better about my English.

✶ 6 ✶

SCIENCE, FINALLY!

I struggle to keep up with all my new schoolwork. An assignment about nouns really confuses me. How am I supposed to know which nouns are proper and which are common?

Don't get me started on commas. I never know where to put them in a sentence.

Sami seems to have a hard time doing his homework too. I hear his loud grumbles each night from my bedroom, even with the door closed.

I miss the old Sami, the one who was always

happy. Back home, we shared a bedroom in our apartment building, and each night, we both listened to the sounds of the Damascus streets dance through our open windows. Sami used to tell shadow puppet stories with his hands against the wall to make me laugh.

Even when we slept in refugee camps and shelters on our way here, Baba's loud snores filled our shared space. It was like a little lullaby to help me fall asleep.

 I wonder if I'll ever get used to the crickets here in Indianapolis.

On Friday, Mrs. James is lining up test tubes on her desk when I walk into class. My face splits into a grin and my steps get quicker. I can smell the science in the air.

"Okay, class, lend me your ears," she says when we all take our seats.

I twirl the ends of my hijab in my hands as I think. No one can lend anyone else their actual ears. Yet another grammar rule I have to learn.

I cover my face with my hands. I'm never going to learn English if words don't even mean what they're supposed to.

Mrs. James claps her hands. "We're going to start with an experiment today. Who can tell me the steps of the scientific method?"

I think hard about our science experiments in Syria, but I can't remember the exact method.

Hannah raises her hand. "Question, Prediction, Observation, Analyzation, and Conclusion."

Mrs. James laughs. "Pretty much. Anyone want to explain?"

Su answers. "You ask a scientific question. Then you make a hypothesis, or what you think is the answer to the question. You conduct the experiment, collect the information, and then analyze it to see what it means. Then you conclude with the results of the experiment."

I feel dizzy from all her fast words.

"Very good," Mrs. James says, her eyes twinkling. "Now, who can guess what our experiment is today?"

I crane my neck to look over the boy in

front of me. Each test tube is filled with little white cubes that look identical. A grin grows on my face. I know what this is; my class did this experiment last year! My hand goes up and Mrs. James points to me.

I open my mouth . . . but the words don't form. It's hard to explain in English. "Ummm, taste food." I stop when I hear the boy in front of me snort.

I shut my mouth quick.

Mrs. James frowns. "Samuel," she says in a warning voice, before turning back to me.

"That's exactly right, Am-eena," she says. "We'll be taste testing, but with a twist."

She walks toward her desk and starts filling the plates with cubes from the tubes. "Who wants to give me a hand?"

Everyone raises their hands.

I jump in my seat and raise mine too. "Can I give my hand? I know!"

I see Tara stifle a smirk from her desk in front, and my hand drops.

"Come on up," Mrs. James says. "Pass out the plates, please."

I give each student a filled paper plate before sliding back into my desk.

"Who wants to make a prediction?" my teacher asks. I twist my head back and forth and look at my classmates, but no one seems to know the answer.

I'm itching to answer, but I don't want to mess up again.

"My sister did a taste experiment at the science fair last year," says Crystal. "She said smell is a bigger part of taste than you would ever guess."

"How?" Mrs. James asks.

I bounce in my seat.

Samuel answers. "Well, good food usually tastes and smells amazing."

"What would happen if you couldn't smell food though, Samuel? Would you know what you were eating?"

"My tongue still works!" he says. The class laughs, but I furrow my eyebrows. That's not the correct answer.

Mrs. James chuckles. "I guess we'll see.

"Okay, class, take a bite," she says. "Now that you have made the hypothesis, conduct the experiment and observe the results. Noses plugged, please."

I pinch my nose and put a cube in my mouth, chewing it just like when we did the experiment last year. Lana giggles. "This is funny!"

Mrs. James turns to the blackboard and

writes: OBSERVATIONS. "What's funny? What did you observe?"

"It tastes like nothing," says Hannah.

"What does that say about smell and taste?"

"They need each other?" says Crystal.

"Exactly," says Mrs. James. "They work together. If your sense of smell is not working, then the sense of taste won't either.

"Can anyone guess what three food items you all ate?"

"Apples?" asks Samuel. "They were crunchy."

"Good, you are using your sense of touch. What else?"

Everyone looks confused.

"Turnips!" says Mrs. James. "And the last cube is . . ."

We lean forward. Mrs. James grins mischievously. "Onions!"

"Ewww . . ." the class says in unison.

"Now for homework . . ." Groans ring out

around the class. Mrs. James continues as if she didn't hear anything. "Make a recipe this weekend and bring your delicious dish to share with us on Monday. Write out the recipe, because you will have to present it to the class before we eat. And remember, write about how your sense of smell affects the taste of your dish!"

My stomach twists into a knot. I can barely string a sentence together. How am I going to stand in front of the class and say a whole speech in English?

⭐ 7 ⭐

AMERICAN APPLE PIE

"What are you going to cook for the class?" Crystal asks me from her seat across the bus aisle.

I put down my pencil and look down at the notebook in my lap.

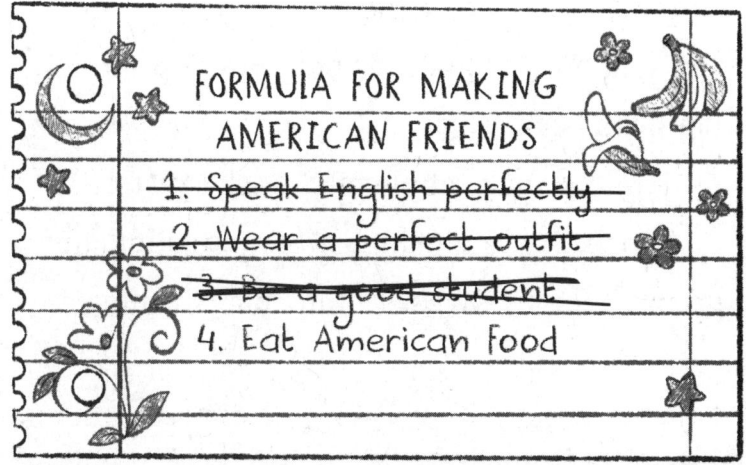

FORMULA FOR MAKING AMERICAN FRIENDS
1. ~~Speak English perfectly~~
2. ~~Wear a perfect outfit~~
3. ~~Be a good student~~
4. Eat American food

I don't know any American foods other than the pasta salad from lunch, and I'm definitely not going to make that.

"What you make?" I ask Crystal hesitantly.

Tara sticks her head in between our seats. "I'm making spaghetti and meatballs. Nothing is more *American* than that!" She narrows her eyes at me as she says *American*, like it's an insult to be anything other than one.

"Well, actually, Tara," Crystal says, "everyone knows the saying is 'Nothing is more American than apple pie.'"

"Whatever." Tara rolls her eyes and moves her head back.

"Are you make apple pie?" I ask Crystal.

"Nope." Crystal laughs. "I'm making my gram's famous sweet potato pie. Nothing is more delicious or more important than a family recipe."

If Crystal isn't making an apple pie, then I'll make one. Maybe if I make a perfect American dish, Tara will finally be nice to me!

I smile as I look outside the bus window at the passing cornfields. If I finish number four in my formula, my experiment for making friends won't be completely ruined after all.

After taking off my shoes, putting them under the bench, and hanging my hijab on one of the coat hooks by the door, I skip to the living room.

"Asalamu alaikum, Mama," I sing out. Mama is changing baby Heba and is also reading a medical textbook that is next to her on the ground. She wipes her eyes, pushes back her bangs, and looks up at me.

"Wa alaikum al salaam, Amina. How was school?" She smiles wide and holds her hands out. I swoop in for a quick hug and bounce back up.

"Alhamdulillah." My answer has been the same for the past four days, but today I say it louder. I have a plan!

"When's Baba coming home?" In Syria, he used to close his pharmacy early so he could cook dinner for us. But here, he's busy making food for other people at the fast-food restaurant where he works.

و عليكم السلام
آمنة
كيف المدرسة ؟

"He still needs a few hours, habibti." I wonder if I should ask Mama to help me make the apple pie instead. But she doesn't like cooking.

Plus, Mama's voice sounds tired. She's been studying for all her doctor tests and taking care of Heba at the same time. In Syria, Tete lived with us, and my grandma took care of my little sister while Mama worked.

But the American papers hadn't counted Tete as part of our family.

Mama finishes putting Heba into a onesie. "I made some freekeh for dinner. Ruhi kilee."

I nod and walk into the kitchen to eat. I grab a bowl, fill it with the green freekeh grains, and sit at the round table, spooning a bite into my mouth.

"Blech." I spit the freekeh out immediately into a napkin. Mama messed up this formula; it's all hard and chewy instead of soft and savory.

I don't want to hurt her feelings, so I carefully put the rest of my freekeh back in the pot before she comes into the kitchen.

My stomach rumbles, so I grab a banana to snack on while I think. How am I going to make an apple pie all by myself?

Mama carries Heba into the kitchen, putting her in her high chair before turning to make a bowl of freekeh mixed with yogurt.

"Can I borrow your phone to look something up?" I ask.

Mama takes it out of her pocket. "Eh khidee, habibti."

I type in: apple pie recipe.

As I scroll through the search engine, I realize there are hundreds of recipes for apple pie. I can't tell which one is the American one.

I retype: American apple pie recipe.

There's still so many. Which one is the *right* one?

I pick the top one and click it. There's a lot of words at the top, so I skip those and go straight to the recipe at the bottom.

I read the list of ingredients. Hmmm . . . flour, cinnamon, sugar, eggs . . . Okay, I think we have those. Ms. Lee had helped Mama stock everything we might need in our kitchen.

I open a cabinet door and take out each item, putting them on the counter. I get the eggs from the fridge. Now I need apples. The recipe asks for ten, but we only have five.

I guess that will have to do.

"What are you making?" Mama asks. She's attempting to spoon-feed Heba, but Heba keeps spitting out the freekeh all over the high chair tray. I hide a smile.

Even my baby sister knows *that* formula for freekeh is wrong!

"An American food for school."

"Okay, let me know if you need help," Mama says, trying a bite from Heba's bowl and grimacing. "Or actually, just wait for your dad."

I let out a laugh and go back to my recipe.

Okay, cutting the apples into slices. That should be easy. I hold the knife carefully like my dad taught me and keep my fingers folded away as I slice.

Now the sugar and lemon juice. We don't

 have measuring cups yet, so I just use a regular cup.

I mix it all together.

Time to make the crust. I crack the eggs over the bowl of flour, making sure to take out any cracked shells that make it in accidentally. Then I add butter slices, slowly, like the recipe says.

Sami walks in the kitchen as I'm trying to roll the dough into a ball. "What is that?"

"American dessert," I tell him confidently.

Sami snorts. "That doesn't look right."

I look down at my hands and the sticky dough on my fingers. He's right. It isn't anything like the picture on the phone.

Maybe some more flour will help. I grab a handful and toss it over the dough.

Sami steps closer to the pot on the stove next to me and sniffs. "Mama cooked?" he whispers to me.

I nod quickly, hoping she doesn't hear him. We've never told her we don't like her food. She didn't really ever cook in Syria, because even when Baba was busy, or Tete didn't make dinner, we would get delicious sandwiches from the street shawarma shop.

Sami sighs.

He looks hopefully at my apple pie. "Are you sure you're following the recipe correctly?"

I'm panting now. I keep adding flour and it's not becoming a nice dough like the picture.

Sami grabs a few apple slices from the bowl next to me and pops them into his mouth. "Mmmm, this is good, at least."

I glare at him and look at my dough. It's become as hard as a rock. I must have added too much flour. The apple pie is ruined.

I feel tears prick my eyes.

"Well, that's definitely not dessert," Sami says.

I brush my arm against my face as hot tears fall from my eyes. I drop the dough, running out of the kitchen and upstairs to the bathroom before anyone sees me crying like a little baby.

✱ 8 ✱

A FUL FOOL

After washing my hands and splashing water on my face, I slowly walk into my bedroom and sit on my bed.

I look down at my list glumly.

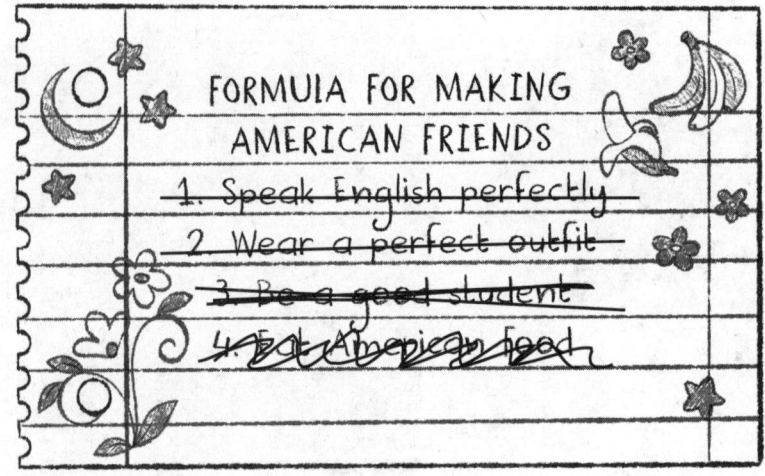

FORMULA FOR MAKING AMERICAN FRIENDS
1. ~~Speak English perfectly~~
2. ~~Wear a perfect outfit~~
3. ~~Be a good student~~
4. ~~Eat American food~~

I'm never going to make American friends. I failed.

I hear a knock at my door and look up.

Mama.

I hurry and hide my paper under my bedspread before she sees it. Her and Baba told us they came here to give us a better life, and here I am messing it all up.

She approaches my bed and sits next to me, her long brown hair flowing over her shoulder. Just like mine does.

Is that why I can't cook? I don't just look like her, but I'm the same in the kitchen.

Mama reaches out a hand to my cheek. "I know that apple recipe isn't the whole problem."

I flatten the space over my hidden paper with my hand.

Mama looks at me, her eyes creasing with worry. "What's bothering you?"

I don't know what to say. Even Arabic can't explain how I feel.

So I shake my head, holding back more tears.

"I know it's hard to move to a new place," Mama says quietly, "but remember, alsabr miftah alfaraj."

Patience is the key to relief.

I smile. One of Tete's sayings. Syrian amtal always mean totally different things than what the words say.

I inhale quickly. Do Americans have amtal too? Is that why words mean totally different things sometimes? I feel like I've cracked a secret code!

Mama traces my smile. "That's what I like to see. Yalla, let's get a snack and clean up. Your dad's going to bring some sandwiches home for us after he finishes up work. That freekeh..."

I giggle and follow my mom downstairs.

Saturday morning, I wake up early to help Baba with breakfast.

I watch him as he washes the soaked ful, adding the beans to the pot on the stove with a pinch of salt. While they boil, he cuts up parsley, tomatoes, and onions into small diced squares. After the beans are soft (he checks with a fork), Baba strains them again and then adds the vegetables on top, garnishing the mix with olive oil, lemon juice, garlic, salt, and cumin spices.

Mama and Heba enter the kitchen. Heba's eyes are bright when she sees the ful, and she laughs and babbles when Mama puts her in the high chair. Heba's a different baby in Indianapolis. She was always wailing on our way out of Syria. She didn't like being unable to play in the refugee tents, and her lips were always trembling no matter how much my mom rocked her. She found leaving Syria scary.

Just like how I felt.

But here, she's happy and smiling. And it makes my heart feel lighter.

Baba slings a hand over my shoulder and says in his heavily accented English, "Don't be a fool, eat some ful." I groan.

Mama giggles, and that's all the encouragement Baba needs. "Ful is perfect *fuel* before a day of hard work." Mama smiles at him, but her eyes dim. I think of how Baba spends his days frying potatoes and chicken nuggets instead of putting together prescriptions like he used to do in Syria.

Sami swaggers in and slumps onto his chair. Heba's happier here in Indianapolis, but Sami's the exact opposite—sullen and quiet.

Mama places fresh pita bread in a basket and sits down. Baba pours her some tea. I close my eyes and inhale the minty smell, and it's almost like I'm back in Tete's kitchen, listening to her tell a story while she plucks mint leaves from a stem and adds them to boiling water.

I tear a piece of warm bread and scoop the ful into my mouth. I chew slowly. If I hadn't seen Baba make it with my own eyes, I would have sworn Mama made it.

"This is delicious, Rami," Mama says.

Baba's eyes are crescent moons. "Sahtein."

Is it only me who thinks this ful tastes different? Even when it smells the same.

Sami opens his mouth. "This ful is weird. Why is everything in America so different?"

"Sami," Mama says, "don't be rude."

"No, he's right," says Baba, chewing thoughtfully. "Something is off about this ful and I haven't been able to figure it out."

"You must have followed the formula wrong," I tell him, thinking of my apple pie.

"Let me look at the ingredients again," Baba says. He stands up and shuffles to the countertop.

What could it be?

"This is definitely parsley," Baba says, holding up green herbs. "It smells the same here."

He sniffs the spices. "Oh yes, this is cumin."

I think of science class. And I think of words in English that sound the same. "What about the ful itself?" I ask. "Sometimes things look the same, but they are actually different."

Baba looks at me. "That could be it." He picks up his phone. I assume he's using his Arabic/English translation app.

Baba's eyes widen as he pulls a bag out of the cabinets. "These are lima beans," he says, "and ful are called fava beans in English."

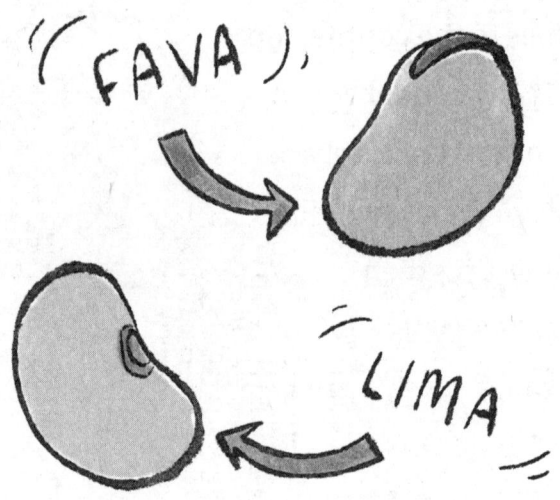

My mouth drops open. "So that's why it tastes different!"

Mama keeps eating. "It tastes good to me." Heba seems to agree, her little fingers putting the ful straight into her mouth, oil dripping down her chin. Mama wipes my sister's mouth with a napkin and Baba chuckles.

Sami shrugs.

"Well, at least we know for next time," I say, finishing my plate. I'm glad we solved this science equation.

Maybe I can solve my friendship formula too.

Maybe.

9

A MASJID REVELATION

A clatter wakes me up. I open my eyes and blink against the bright sunlight as Mama slides open the curtains of my bedroom window. "Get up, Amina, you need to get ready for school."

I yawn and look at the clock. "Mama, it's Sunday."

"First day of Islamic school at the masjid, remember?" Mama says. I throw off my covers immediately and jump up. Fatima told me she would see me there!

I wonder if masjids here have the same

curving Arabic calligraphy on the outside and tall, proud minarets stretching into the sky that the ones in Syria do.

I make wudu in the bathroom, following the steps of washing my face, arms, and feet to get ready for prayer, and then pull a comb through my hair. After I dress into my hijab and abaya, I smooth a hand over my long dress and look in the mirror. I look just like I did before Jummah prayers in Syria, and a happy glow fills my chest.

Mama parks the car and looks back at us. "Ready?"

"Are you sure this is the masjid?" I ask, looking out at the plain, boxy brown building in front of us.

Mama nods. "It's the address your dad gave me."

We had to drop Baba off at his work first, because he and Mama share a car. This is the first time we've come to the masjid, even though Baba prays Jummah here each Friday.

Heba's pushing against the restraints in her car seat next to me, excited to get out, but I can hear Sami's grumbles from the back.

I wish he would stop complaining about everything. It's hard for all of us; Syria was home. We all miss it.

I take a deep breath and smile at Mama. "Let's go."

We open the glass doors and walk into

the lobby. I hear the Athan being called on the loudspeakers for Dhuhr prayer, and the familiarity soothes me. The same words are repeated in Syria, and no matter where I go in the world, I pray the same prayers and face the same direction.

I look up at Mama and see the peaceful smile on her face, mirroring my own. She squeezes my shoulder. We take off our shoes, placing them on the shoe rack, and make our way inside.

Sami heads to the men's side and we walk toward the other women. I wave at Fatima, and she jumps up from the plush carpet, grabbing a woman I assume is her mom and dragging her to us. "Salaam, Amina. You came," she says, hugging me. Our mothers greet each other, and we sit to wait for prayer to start.

The imam stands to ask everyone to make more room for those coming in, and I

furrow my brow. His words are in English, but they sound different.

"Is he new too?" I ask Fatima.

She looks confused. "No, Imam Mohammad has been at our masjid since I was a baby."

"Why does he talk differently in English?" I whisper to her.

"Oh!" Fatima looks like she's holding back a laugh. "He's from Boston! Some Americans have different accents. You should hear how my cousins talk when they visit from Texas. They have a Southern accent, and it's so cool."

People in America have different accents while talking English?

I think of my list at home. Maybe I shouldn't have put speaking English perfectly as number one if Americans speak differently.

I remember number four on the list. Maybe Fatima will have ideas for American foods easier to make than apple pie.

"Have you decided what to make for Monday?" I ask.

Fatima grins. "I'm bringing in koshary! It's my favorite food."

My jaw drops. "You're taking an Egyptian food to class?"

Fatima gives me a strange look. "Yeah. Why not?"

The Iqamah sounds out of the front, the muathen making the second call to prayer into the microphone. I lean toward Fatima.

"So we don't have to make American foods?"

Fatima frowns. "Koshary *is* American if I'm making it."

I'm about to ask more questions when I see Mama. She's giving me a warning glance from the carpet where she's sitting with Heba.

We aren't supposed to talk once the Iqamah is called.

I close my mouth and stand up with Fatima to pray.

We stand side by side, shoulder to shoulder, everyone bowing their heads together and murmuring the same verses from the Quran. When we kneel to the ground and I press my head to the plush carpet, I feel at home.

My heart warms, and I forget everything and just focus on this feeling of belonging.

After prayer, we gather in a circle for our Quran classes with the imam. He asks me to read aloud, and as the beautiful melodic words flow from my mouth, I see everyone's mouths open in awe.

He beams at me. "Your Arabic recitation is perfect!" A kind warmth flows through my body.

As I sit next to Fatima, my Quran in my hands, I realize that it doesn't matter what the masjid looks like on the outside.

On the inside, it feels perfect.

✦ 10 ✦

AMINA BANANA

When we get home, the first thing I do is toss my formula list in the garbage. Some experiments can't be controlled, and I was doing it all wrong, anyways.

I sit next to Mama while she studies at the kitchen table. I have my notebook, and she has her medical books.

My report is due tomorrow, and I've decided what I want to make.

Ful!

I try to remember as much of Baba's recipe

as I can from this morning and write it down in English.

I write, and erase.

I write a few words, and erase again.

I write, then I erase so hard I rip through the notepaper. I crumple the paper and toss it into the trash. "*Gah!* English is so hard."

Mama looks up from her book. "I know."

My mouth drops open. "You think it's hard too? But you're so smart!"

Mama smiles. "Being smart has nothing to do with how hard something is. It comes from trying your best, even when it's difficult." Mama flips a page in the thick book in front of her and highlights a passage.

I think of how we had to leave our home. How my parents heard that they might be taken to jail, just for helping treat people who were injured.

People who asked for the country to be free. And the Syrian government didn't like that.

"Do you wish we could have stayed in Syria?" I ask her. "You wouldn't have to take your doctor tests all over again." *And no one would make fun of my accent in English.*

"Hmm," says Mama. "I try not to think of what could have been. We can't control what happens in life. We have to trust in Allah and try our best to move forward the best we can."

I see Sami freeze as he grabs a snack from the fridge.

I pick up my pencil again and focus on my paper. Mama's right. Bismillah.

The next morning, I wake up extra early. I cook the ful myself, but this time with all of the right ingredients. Baba's working next to me to make sure I don't burn myself, helping me drain the boiling water. But he doesn't really help me *that* much.

I do it all myself!

Mama's filling out applications for her boards at the table while rocking baby Heba with her legs. She sings the Syrian nursery rhyme:

> *Hizil tute ya tawat*
> *tootak shame ya tawat*

The Arabic words about Syrian berries swirl around me as I poke the ful, and for a second, when I close my eyes and the garlicky-lemon smell fills my nose, everything feels just right.

Sami walks into the kitchen. He reaches in front of me as I'm chopping the tomatoes and grabs an apple from the fruit basket.

"Wow," he tells me. "That looks good."

"I think the tomato cubes are too big," I tell him, squinting at the pieces.

"It doesn't mean if things are different that they can't be good too."

The kitchen is quiet. I look at Sami and smile. "You're right!"

My older brother smiles back at me and says salaam before he leaves for his bus. It comes a little earlier than mine.

I hurry to finish the rest of my recipe.

"Did you schedule your test?" I hear Baba ask Mama.

"Not yet," she says. "Soon, insha Allah."

Baba's hands hug Mama's shoulders and she leans back, closing her eyes. I remember how Baba had taken the pharmacy exams right when we got here, but he wasn't able to pass. He decided to get a job to support us while Mama studied.

I raise my hands to the sky and make a silent prayer. "May Allah help Mama pass her tests."

I finish garnishing the ful with tomatoes and parsley, and the smell that reaches my nose is a delicious garden of Syrian goodness.

Baba looks at the dish. "It looks perfect!"

"It is," I say, smiling to myself. A small splash of Syria in America.

"The true test is the taste," he tells me, winking as he grabs a spoon from the drawer and dips it into the fava bean mix.

I wrap the ful platter in foil.

I don't need to look at Baba to know this was a successful experiment. I can hear his hums as the ful hits his tongue follow me all the way out the front door.

"What is that smell?" Tara says and sticks out her tongue, pretending to choke when I get on the bus. I ignore her and sit next to Crystal, who's holding a sweet potato pie. The fragrance makes my mouth water.

"Did you write your report?" Crystal asks.

"Yes." I pull it out. I had written and erased so many times, the paper looked frayed. "It took long time."

Crystal rolls her eyes. "You can say that again."

"It took long time," I say again. Tara lets out a mocking giggle from behind me.

Crystal holds out her hand. "Let me take a look," she says. I hold my breath.

"Wow," she says. "This is awesome, Ameena."

"Sank—I mean th-ank you," I tell her.

Then I clear my throat. "That's not how to say my name." I close my eyes as my heart races in my chest. What if she gets mad at me for telling her?

"Oh! How do you say your name?" she asks.

I look down at my favorite snack in my lap. "Amina is said kind of like *banana*."

She grins. "Amina Banana, I love it!"

"My last name actually means *banana* in Arabic," I say, a little louder, braver.

"No way!" says Crystal. "Amina Banana has a nice ring to it."

I like jewelry, and especially rings, and I decide I like my new nickname too.

When we get to school, I get off the bus with quick, light steps.

… 11 …

THE FINAL INGREDIENT

Mrs. James takes each plate of food as we walk in. She places them on a long table in the front of her desk and asks us to take our seats.

"I am excited to hear all the presentations and taste the results of your experiments. And this time, you all can use your noses too. No, Samuel, not to eat with, but to smell with."

I giggle. Mrs. James is way better than Ms. Frizzle.

"Who wants to start?" she asks. Crystal raises her hand.

One by one, my classmates give their presentations about their recipes. Hannah shares latkes, and they smell like crispy potato goodness. Fatima shares Egyptian koshary, which is a mix of fragrant lentils, pasta, and rice. Lana shares kibbeh, and the scent reminds me of home. Su shows us a plate of gimbap, which look like delicious rainbow sushi circles. Crystal's sweet potato pie is a huge hit in the class, and she shows us a picture of her grandma and her making it together. Tara's spaghetti makes my mouth water. Bella's banana bread makes me excited! Even Samuel's presentation is fun, with peanut butter and jelly

sandwiches cut into small
football shapes.

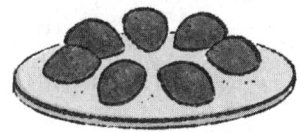

Everyone does such a
good job in English, their words flowing like
smooth poetry out of their mouths.

When it's my turn, I freeze.

Am I really ready to talk loudly in front of
the class in English? I had practiced last night
over and over in front of my mirror until my
words sounded right. But with the eyes of my
classmates on me, my tongue feels stuck. Mrs.
James motions me forward.

"Break a leg, Am-eena," she says.

"It's Aah-mina, kinda like banana," I hear
Crystal tell my teacher,
but her voice
sounds far away,
and my heart is
pounding in
my ears.

My legs are shaking. They certainly feel like they're about to break. Is that what the American saying means? Being so nervous, you can't move?

Mrs. James notices me looking at my legs. "It means I hope you do a good job, Amina," she says, winking. She pats my shoulder and steps to the side.

Crystal gives me a thumbs-up, and my heart lifts as I look at the encouraging faces of all my new friends.

I hold my paper up, take a deep breath, and begin to read.

"Ful mdamas is Syrian breakfast made of fava beans. You boil beans in water until soft, then drain. You add tomatoes, onions, parsley over it in bowl. Then you squeeze lemon, mash garlic over, and season with salt and cumin. The last and most important part is *lots* of olive oil, which we put in every Syria dish.

"When my dad making ful here in America, it was tasting wrong. So, I figure out that formula must be fixed, because cooking like science. My hypothesis was that ingredient had to be wrong, but everything look the same as ingredients in Syria. Since things can look same, and smell same, but taste different, I examine the ingredients until we discovered ful my dad was using was lima beans, not fava beans. That was problem, and fixing it fixed recipe.

"Now when I eat ful, it tastes perfect again. And it reminds me of my home."

I hurry back to my seat, my throat dry from all the talking. My stomach rolls, but my body feels light. *I did it!* Mrs. James claps, and the rest of the class follows. "That was perfect, Amina!

Okay, class," she says, "who's ready to eat?"

Everyone raises their hands.

We stand in a line, filling our plates with different foods. The colors and flavors and smells might be different, but all of it is located on one table together. It makes me smile a wide banana smile.

Tara stops in front of the koshary. She sniffs. "What is *that*?"

Fatima is at the front of the line. She looks back, and I see her eyes widen. She looks hurt. And before I know it, my mouth is open and I'm talking in English.

"That food is koshary," I say loudly. "And it is really yummy."

Tara doesn't respond. Everyone rushes to put koshary on their plates.

Fatima smiles at me as we make our way to our seats.

Hannah licks her lips as she takes the first bite. "This ful is amazing."

Su turns to me. "I need more Syrian recipes! You got to spill the beans." I'm not sure why she would want me to spill the ful. But I don't want to offend my new friend, and so I tilt my plate. The beans go everywhere and Su's mouth drops open. I can hear Tara laughing.

"I didn't mean to spill the actual beans. I just want you to share the recipe." Crystal and Lana hand me napkins, and Su helps me wipe up the spilled ful.

"It must be confusing for you to hear all these phrases," says Fatima.

"We'll try to explain better," says Crystal. My flaming face cools.

"Here, you can share my plate," Lana says after my desk is clean.

I take a bite of banana bread and sigh. "This delicious, Bella. It bananas and cake all together."

Bella grins. "It was easy! I didn't solve a whole food mystery like you did, though."

"That's way cool," agrees Su.

Crystal sighs. "If only you could fix the cafeteria lunch formula too, Amina Banana."

Lana snorts, and we burst out laughing. As we dig into our food, I look around and smile.

I didn't need a formula to make American friends!

Making American friends is just like making Syrian friends. Just like I first became friends with Judy, when we were both in preschool and I shared my crayons with her during art class.

The only ingredient is being kind.

⭐ EXTRAS! ⭐

THE STEPS OF MRS. JAMES'S SCIENTIFIC METHOD

Hello, science lovers! Have an experiment idea?

To perform any science experiment, you must first follow the steps of the scientific method.

1. Figure out your question. What is the problem you want to solve?

2. Make a hypothesis—a prediction based on the data you know. What do you think is the answer?

3. Perform the experiment. (Remember, ask an adult for help, especially with anything hot or dangerous!)

4. Write down your observations.

5. Think about the data you collected and the results you observed.

6. Make a conclusion! Does it match up to your prediction?

And of course, share your results with others!

AN EXPERIMENT ON SMELL AND TASTE

The experiment that Amina performs in her class with Mrs. James is the experiment of smell and taste and how they are connected. To try this fun experiment yourself, gather the items needed and get a friend for help!

ITEMS:

- 1 raw turnip, apple, and onion (have an adult cut each into small cubes)
- Paper plates
- A friend

EXPERIMENT:

Conduct this experiment using the steps of the scientific method outlined.

1. Figure out the question. How are smell and taste connected?

2. Make a hypothesis. Write down what you think about smell and taste in a notebook. Do you think you can guess the taste of a food item if you don't smell it?

3. Perform the experiment. Have a friend, or adult, put identical-looking cubes from the apple, onion, and turnip on three plates and mix them up without you looking. Plug your nose with your two fingers and take a bite, trying to guess what it is you are eating.

4. Write down your observations. Do they taste the same or different?

5. Now try the experiment again with your nose unplugged. Is the data you collected different or the same?

6. Think about your data. What does it say about taste and smell?

7. Make a conclusion. How do taste and smell work together to make food taste delicious?

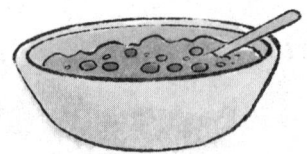

AMINA'S FUL MDAMAS RECIPE

Make sure to cook with an adult present, especially for cutting with sharp utensils and using the stove!

MAKES ONE BOWL OF FUL, ABOUT 5-6 SERVINGS
PREP TIME: 30 MIN-1 HOUR

ITEMS:

- 1 16 oz bag of dried fava beans, soaked and submerged overnight in water
- 1 large tomato, diced into small cubes
- 1 large onion, diced into small cubes
- 3 cloves of garlic, mashed
- 1 lemon, squeezed

- 1 tablespoon of salt, and more to taste
- 1 tablespoon of cumin, and more to taste
- ½ cup of olive oil, and as needed
- 2 small bunches of Italian parsley, finely chopped

INSTRUCTIONS:

1. Drain and rinse the soaked fava beans. Put them in a pot and cover with water. Boil for about an hour or until the ful is soft when poked with a fork.

2. Drain the ful and place it in a bowl. Lightly mash it with a fork until the ful is still somewhat bean-shaped but also soft.

3. Add the tomatoes and onions over the ful, and mix gently with a serving spoon.

4. Add the garlic, lemon juice, one tablespoon of salt, and one tablespoon of cumin. Mix gently, avoiding mashing the beans completely.

5. Add ½ cup of olive oil.

6. Fold half the parsley into the ful by stirring with the spoon gently until the parsley is evenly mixed.

7. Garnish the platter of ful with the rest of the parsley.

8. Taste, and add olive oil and cumin as preferred.

9. Serve into small bowls and enjoy with pita bread on the side!

A Note from the Author About the Syrian Refugee Crisis

Amina and her family are fictional characters, but their situation is not made up. The Syrian refugee crisis is the largest refugee crisis in the world. Since 2011, over six million people (and growing) are estimated to have fled Syria in search for safety, housing, food, and water, with another six million people displaced inside of Syria.

The Ba'ath-controlled Syrian government, led by Bashar al-Assad until December 8, 2024, was responsible for the violence that displaced many Syrians. Many fled into neighboring countries like Türkiye, Lebanon, and Jordan. A large number of refugees, like Amina and her family, had to ride in flimsy boats, then walk for hours in new countries until they were accepted into a new home. Refugees must apply for resettlement, and papers can take a long time to be approved.

And even though the overthrow of Bashar al-Assad's government sparked a lot of hope for Syrians, the scars of his cruelty are still etched in so many lives.

Sadly, children are the main group affected by the war. When the conflict in Syria began, many schools shuttered. Syrian children have endured brutal sounds of war and witnessed violence, which has caused a mental health crisis. Medical professionals who help Syrian revolutionaries are targeted, and have to flee, like Amina's parents.

Adult refugees like Amina's parents struggle to use their college degrees in other countries, as Syrians study in Arabic, and oftentimes, it is difficult to pass testing in a new language. With financial insecurity and unemployment problems, children who are refugees do not have their basic needs met. As they settle in a new country, like the United States, the hope for many refugees is that the next generation will be able to grow up in a better environment, and have a better, safer future.

Acknowledgments

Alhamdulillah to the Creator and Gift-Giver, who has given me so much, who has allowed me to follow my dream of being a storyteller and provided me with the ability to serve my community. I am so grateful for this blessing.

Thank you to The Word, A Storytelling Sanctuary, who offered a mentorship that allowed me the opportunity to work with the incredible Rūta Rimas on this chapter book. Alyssa Reynoso-Morris, I will never forget that first phone call where you told me my manuscript was chosen. Thank you for laughing when I squealed with happiness, and I am sorry to your poor ears for my uncontrollable, very LOUD excitement!

Thank you to my brilliant editor Rūta Rimas, who is not only a fabulous magic-maker with words but also a pleasure to work with! I am so honored to make beautiful books with you.

Thank you to wonderful editor Simone Roberts-Payne, whose insights are just as bright as sunshine!

Thank you to my amazing agent, Janine Le, who is always supportive and encouraging and believes in my words and work so strongly! I couldn't ask for a better champion.

Thank you to Aaliya Jaleel for the amazing art and infusing soul into the words of Amina Banana. I am so happy to partner with you on so many beautiful books.

Thank you to Rye White; Kristie Radwilowicz; Rebecca Aidlin; Abigail Powers; Jen Klonsky; Nancy Mercado; my publicist, Sierra

Pregosin; the incredible School and Library team (Carmela, Trevor, Summer, and more); the Penguin socials team (Tolani and Lauren); and so many others who help usher stunning stories into the world of kidlit. You all are so wonderful!

Thank you to my husband, T, who has not only been an incredible partner, but the very reason I am able to pursue my dream of writing so fully. Thank you for all you do for our family! You are an answer to a duaa and one I am so very glad got answered!

Thank you to my beautiful kiddos for always being so excited every time I write a new book. I hope you always find pride and confidence in who you are!

Thank you to my parents, who came to America and brought me with them as a little girl. I know it must have been hard, moving to a new home, learning a new language, trying to navigate a new culture—but you both did it with such strength and grace and love. I hope you are so proud of the writer, and human, you both shaped me to be!

Thank you so much to my dear friend Kirin Nabi for always being so supportive and telling me that the world needs more Syrian stories—and believing in the importance and beauty of the ones I tell (and reading them over and over and loving them every time).

Thank you to reviewers and booksellers and librarians and educators—you all are the best!

And thank YOU, dear reader, for picking up this book and reading these words. I hope you find beauty and love in them—they came from my whole heart!

READ THE FIRST CHAPTER OF

BOOK TWO OF THE AMINA BANANA SERIES!

Amina Banana's class is abuzz with excitement for the upcoming spelling bee! But spelling in English is tough for Amina. Still, she's going to prove to her classmates that even if English is an additional language for her, she can take home the gold medal.

If only the formula for winning weren't so complicated!

✦ 1 ✦

SWIMMING WORDS

I clasp my pencil tightly and look around the classroom. Everyone's focused on their papers, but I am frozen at my desk.

Fridays are supposed to be the best day of the week, a day of planning fun for the weekend. In Syria, everyone had Fridays off to go to Jummah, and we ate sweets after prayers.

But here in America, I'm in school, and I dread this day the most. And it's all because of one reason.

Spelling.

I had spent the last four days of the week avoiding the long list of words I was supposed to memorize. But now, every time Mrs. James opens her mouth to recite a spelling word, my mind goes blank. Ah, and the definitions!

As if Mrs. James explaining what the word means will somehow help me "magically remember" how to spell it.

I try to listen closely as Mrs. James says each word, imagining the letters in my mind. But then the test is over, my teacher is

finished speaking, the words are swimming in my brain, and angry slashes from my pencil are scattered all over the paper.

I bite my lip as Mrs. James steps closer and closer to my desk. Everyone's giving her their tests, and no one looks worried. No one notices my head is spinning, not even my friends Lana and Crystal.

I see Tara writing her name on the top of hers with a flourish, as if she's signing an award for the best speller in America.

I can already imagine the huge star I'll see on her test Monday from where I sit behind her.

I always get red marks, and a note at the top saying: *Better luck next time.*

But it's not luck that I'm awful at spelling. It's that I came to Indiana a few weeks ago, and I'm still struggling to keep up with all the English everyone has been learning their whole life.

Shoes stop by my desk. I look up.

Mrs. James smiles and holds out a hand,

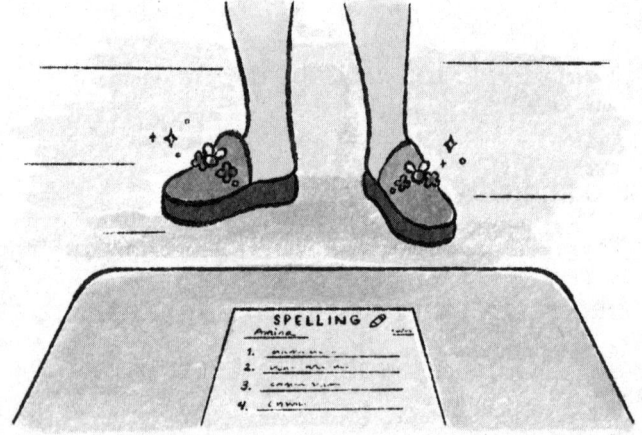

but my fingers tighten on my paper. Maybe if I check my words again, they'll mysteriously morph into the right spelling.

"Are you okay, Amina?" my teacher asks. Her eyes fill with concern.

I look away, shame rising in my chest. Mrs. James leans forward and gently pries my test out of my clenched fingers.

"Don't worry," she says, patting my shoulder as she moves past me. But how am I not supposed to worry when I know I did horrible?

"Time to get ready for dismissal," Mrs. James announces.

Squeaks sound against the ground as everyone gets up, pushes their chairs to their desk, and begins to pack their bags.

"Whew, I'm dead," Crystal says from next to me. I look sideways at my friend, trying to figure out what she means. She looks perfectly alive to me.

Crystal notices my look and smirks. "It means I'm tired, Amina Banana."

"I knew that." I let out a chuckle.

The truth is that these American phrases are tricky for me to understand, even after a month in my new home. And even though my friends try to explain, it still makes me feel out of place when everyone understands these jokes but me.

I open my bookbag, making sure my notebooks are neatly placed behind my folders, and zip up.

Crystal shows me a book. "I can't believe the librarian managed to snag me the seventh Unicorn Universe book. It's sold out everywhere!" She squeals as she hugs the chapter book to her chest.

"Is librarian nice?" I ask, then make my voice low so no one else can hear. "Mrs. James told me I going to do English as a Second Language with her," I admit.

"You should ask her to borrow the first Unicorn Universe book when you're doing that extra English class!" Crystal's loud voice makes me wince. She doesn't realize I don't

want anyone else to know about my special lessons.

Tara's bookbag bumps into my shoulder as she turns, and I grimace. I hope she didn't overhear. It'll be just one other reason for her to point out how different I am from everyone else.

"I knew you needed help in English," she says. "You talk all wrong. My aunt's going to straighten you out quick."

I imagine my body being stretched into a straight line. My eyes widen. "The librarian is Tara's aunt?"

"Don't worry," says Crystal. "It'll be a piece of cake."

Cake is delicious.

But I'm not so sure about ESL class.

I stay silent the whole bus ride home.